The Steam Tr

Written by Ian Whybrow
Illustrated by Rosalind Hudson

Gosh,
I wish
I were a bus,

It's much less work
And much less fuss.

I should like that,
I should like that.

De-deedle-dee
De-diddle-dum,
Just look at me
'Cause here I come.

Pain in my back, aches in my joints,
Tickerty-tack, here are the points.

Diddly-dee, diddly dee,
Diddly WIDDLY diddly dee!

Far to go? Not very far.
Little black tunnel ...
... Tickerty WHAAAH!

And now I'd better slow right down,
In half a mile we reach the town.

Then you'll paddle and splash in the sea,
And have ice cream and cake for tea.

But gosh I'm tired,
Oh gosh I'm tired,
Hohhh
GOSSSSSSSSSSSSSHHHHHHHHHHHHHH

Ideas for guided reading

Learning objectives: use syntax and context when reading for meaning; identify the main events and characters in stories, and find specific information in simple texts; explore the effect of patterns of language and repeated words and phrases; interpret a text by reading aloud with some variety in pace and emphasis

Curriculum links: Music: Feel the pulse

High frequency words: I, were, a, much, and, should, like, that, just, look, at, me, here, come, in, my, back, are, the, to, go, not, very, little, black, what, there, now, down, half, we, then, have, for, but

Interest words: aches, joints, points, tunnel, paddle, splash

Word count: 116

Resources: percussion instruments, paper and pens

Getting started

- Ask children if they have been on a steam train and what they know about steam trains from other stories and television programmes.

- As a group, make the noises that a steam train can make, e.g. *diddly-dee diddly dah*. Practise getting faster and slower.

- Look at the covers. Read the title and the blurb to the children. Emphasise the rhythm of the poem's blurb.

- Reread the blurb aloud as a group, emphasising the rhythm.

Reading and responding

- Ask children to read pp2–3 in pairs, practising making the words sound like the train's engine.

- Ask children to predict where the train might be going and what might happen on the way.

- In pairs, ask children to read to p13, working out how to make the train sound slow and then fast and then slow again. Support children as they work together, especially with tricky sound words like *de-deedle-dee*.